The Biggest House in the World

by Leo Lionni

Pantheon

Some snails lived on a juicy cabbage.
They moved gently around, carrying their houses
from leaf to leaf, in search of
a tender spot to nibble on.

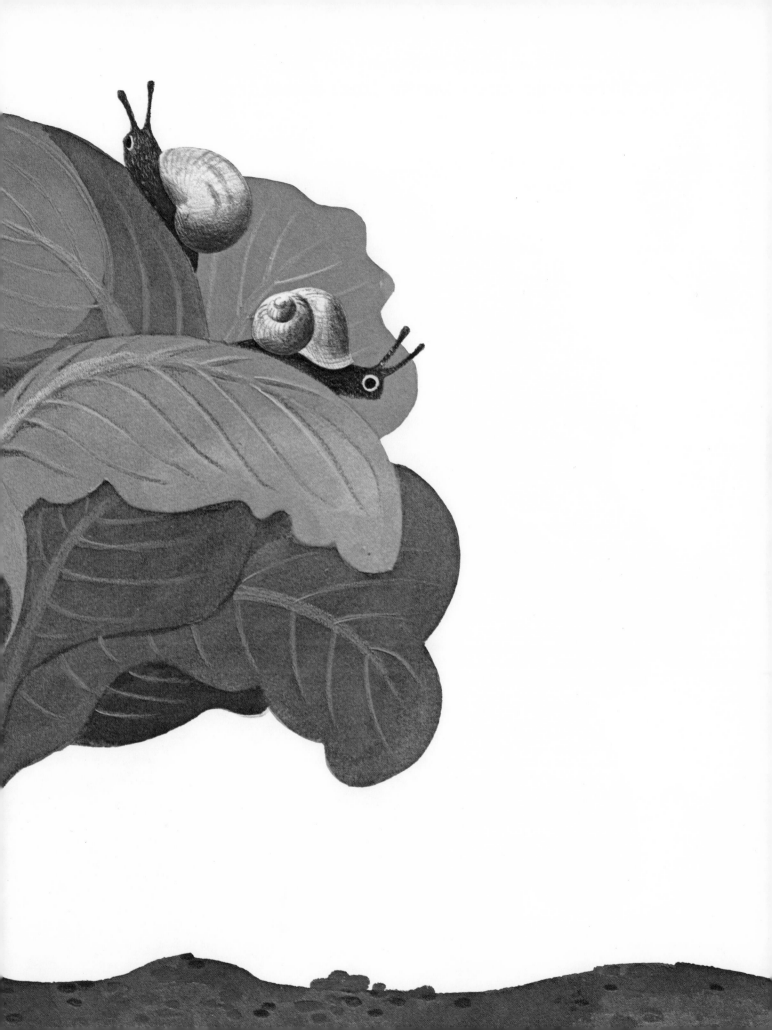

One day a little snail said to his father,
"When I grow up I want to have the biggest house in the world."
"That is silly," said his father,
who happened to be the wisest snail on the cabbage.
"Some things are better small."
And he told this story.

Once upon a time, a little snail, just like you,
said to his father, "When I grow up
I want to have the biggest house in the world."
"Some things are better small," said his father.
"Keep your house light and easy to carry."

But the little snail would not listen, and
hidden in the shade of a large cabbage leaf, he twisted and twitched,
this way and that, until he discovered how to make his house grow.

It grew and grew, and the snails on the cabbage said,
"You surely have the biggest house in the world."

The little snail kept on twisting and twitching
until his house was as big as a melon.

Then, by moving his tail swiftly from left to right,
he learned to grow large pointed bulges.

And by squeezing and pushing, and by wishing very hard, he was able to add bright colors and beautiful designs.

Now he knew that his was the biggest and the
most beautiful house in the whole world.
He was proud and happy.

A swarm of butterflies flew overhead.
"Look!" one of them said. "A cathedral!"
"No," said another, "it's a circus!"
They never guessed that what they were looking at
was the house of a snail.

And a family of frogs, on their way to a distant pond,
stopped in awe. "Never," they later told some cousins,
"never have you seen such an amazing sight.
An ordinary little snail with a house like a birthday cake."

One day after they had eaten all the leaves
and only a few knobby stems were left,
the snails moved to another cabbage.
But the little snail, alas, couldn't move.
His house was much too heavy.

He was left behind, and with nothing to eat
he slowly faded away. Nothing remained but the house.
And that too, little by little, crumbled,
until nothing remained at all.

That was the end of the story. The little snail was almost in tears.

But then he remembered his own house.
"I shall keep it small," he thought,
"and when I grow up I shall go wherever I please."

And so one day, light and joyous, he went on to see the world.
Some leaves fluttered lightly in the breeze,
and others hung heavily to the ground.
Where the dark earth had split, crystals glittered in
the early sun. There were polka-dotted mushrooms,
and towery stems from which little flowers seemed to wave.
There was a pinecone lying in the lacy shade of ferns,
and pebbles in a nest of sand, smooth and round
like the eggs of the turtledove. Lichen clung
to the rocks and bark to the trees.
The tender buds were sweet and cool with morning dew.
The little snail was very happy.

The seasons came and went,
but the snail never forgot the story his father had told him.
And when someone asked, "How come you have such a small house?"
he would tell the story of
the biggest house in the world.